I Am One with G-d

STORY BY
BOB CUTLER

WRITTEN BY
MEGAN LANGFORD

ILLUSTRATED BY
HAYLEY CLEARY

With special thanks to Junior Art Director, Megan Wyatt, Creative Director, Bryan Sedey, and Project Coodinators, Kaylea Ford and Brooke Rodina.

To Bodhi

I Am One with G-d

How can we ensure that our children feel loved, embraced, and accepted? We live in a very insecure world where it is so easy to feel small and insignificant. How can we feel anything but anxiety, panic, and insecurity when we feel so vulnerable? This is the gift of this book, "I Am One with G-d".

Within these pages we implant within the hearts and minds of our children (and ourselves!) the powerful idea that at our core we all possess a pure G-dly soul. This essential part of our being is who we really are. It runs much deeper than the color of our skin and our own self-perception that is often based on the external layers of ourselves.

As you read this book, open up your heart to be fully aware that deep within we are truly one with G-d and therefore one with all of creation. As we instill this idea within ourselves and our children, we will no longer feel alone, insecure, or afraid. Because even in the darkest of times; "I Am One with G-d."

A note about the word "G-d": Treating G-d's name with reverence is a way to give respect to Him. According to tradition, the various names for our Creator are all considered holy and must be treated with the utmost respect. It is therefore traditional to insert the dash in place of spelling out the English term used to translate G-d's holy name.

~Rabbi Zalman Tiechtel

Look in the mirror . . . What do you see?

What kind of person do you want to be?

Thoughtful and caring, and braver than brave
with a heart full of love and a brain full of waves.
All of these things are inside you, you know.
Your Maker will guide you as you find your glow!

Be kind to yourself
(though that can be tough).
You were made perfectly,
and you are enough.

Good enough, smart enough,
kind enough, too.
Tall enough, fast enough,
with just the right shoes.

That doesn't mean that each day will be easy.

Your cereal's too soggy or your pizza's not cheesy.

Even on days when you just want to hide,
you're still the same person way deep down inside.
Each day can be different—some smiles and some frowns—
and even the grown-ups have big ups and downs.

Sometimes you're grumpy or grouchy and tired.

Another day cheerful, excited, and wired.

All of your feelings are perfect. It's true!
But they don't define who you are—
the REAL you.

The way that you look or the way that you're viewed—
the language you speak or your favorite snack food . . .

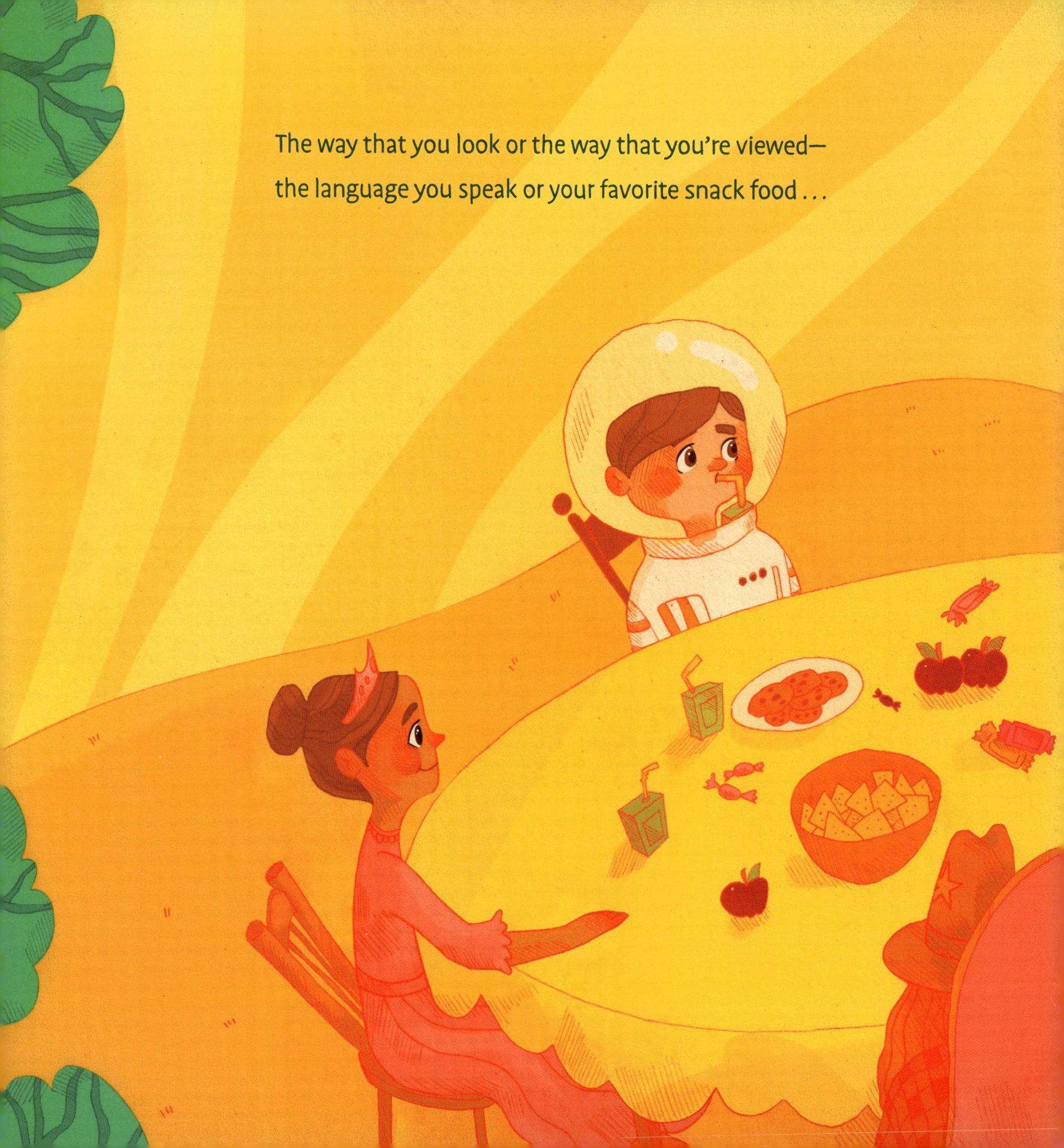

These bits and pieces don't make you complete.
There's something inside that's really quite neat.

That something's more precious than gold in a vault,
and we need it more than popcorn needs salt.
Whatever we're feeling, however we look...

The Divine lives within each cranny and nook.

Our differences aren't all that different, you see.

There's one thing we all have that sets us all free.

We are connected by a spirit inside.

It's in every person the whole world wide.

"The whole world wide?" you say. "But how?"

"I don't even know all my neighbors right now."

The world is so big and full of unknowns

But your Maker is with you—you're never alone.

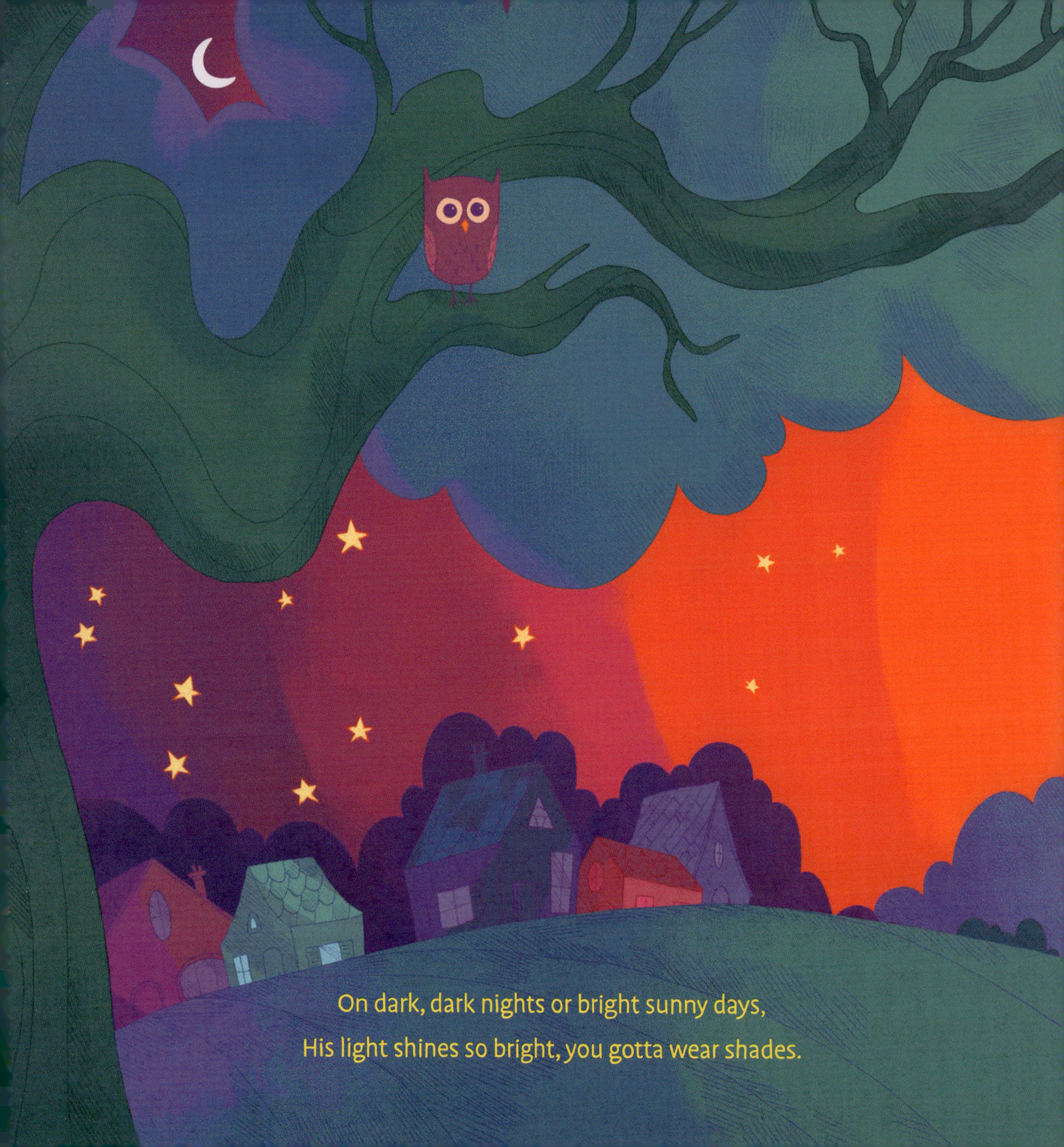

On dark, dark nights or bright sunny days,
His light shines so bright, you gotta wear shades.

That light's all around us. It shines super bright!

It brings us together and makes everything right.

Remember that light if things ever go dark.
We're all connected by the very same spark.

Your brother, your sister, that kid down the street
and all of the other people you meet—
They've all got worries, and everyone doubts.
But we all have a light that can never go out.

Let your light shine
for the whole world to see.
Shout it out,

"I am LOVED by the one who made ME!"

Even on the worst days, don't worry. Take heart.

Each day you wake up, you get a fresh start

to look in that mirror again and be awed . . .

And say to yourself,

"I AM ONE WITH G-D!"

This book belongs to

_____

This book is a gift from

_____